Annette

Being bad
feels so good!

Maureen

MIAMI HUSH CLUB

NOVELLA - EPISODE 1

MICHELLE WARREN

MIAMI HUSH CLUB

Editing and Formatting by:

Pam Berehulke

www.BulletproofEditing.com

Cover and Book Design by:

Michelle Preast

www.facebook.com/indiebookcovers

READER WARNING

If you have any emotional triggers, please do not read this book.

This book is for readers 18+. It contains strong language, cheating, sex, violence, disturbing and immoral behavior, and more.

• • •

Before I started, I knew the plot points of this story, but I didn't know what the souls of these characters would be composed of. Good or bad, I let them tell me who they were as I wrote. And what I discovered was that with their imperfect lives, they preferred to be dark and twisted.

THIS SERIES

Miami Hush Club - Novella - Episode 1 (Releases Jan. 19, 2015)

Miami Hush Club - Novella - Episode 2 (Releases Jan. 26, 2015)

Miami Hush Club - Novella - Episode 3 (Releases Feb. 2, 2015)

Miami Hush Club - Novella - Episode 4 (Releases Feb. 9, 2015)

• I do not recap with each novella, so please read books in order. •

CONTENTS

Nicolette

Girls like me don't get happily-ever-afters. At least, I considered it impossible until I met Casper. He charmed me with his stunning smile, protected my secrets with his strong arms, and melded my fragmented heart with his own, until I gave him every piece of me.

With the naïveté of a child, I hoped for a future together, but I should have known better. I should have been on my guard.

Ten years ago

The moment playing out before my eyes is ripe with irony.

My boyfriend is having sex, but not with me. Even though we run a wildly successful escort service together, I expected Casper to be faithful. What a lovesick fool I was. Instead, it's me who's being fucked as I helplessly watch my sister and best escort, Alex, sit atop Casper's dick, enthusiastically riding him into next week.

At first I'm frozen in shock, so the situation crashing down on me is momentarily unfathomable. In some ways, it's a nightmare that makes no sense.

My heart stops, collapsing in my chest and sinking into my gut as I desperately try to hold myself upright. Or maybe those are my malfunctioning lungs, unable to inhale the thickness of betrayal-laced air. Either way, it's only my vision that continues working. My eyes soak up all the information, piecing together fragments of incomprehensible images as my brain tries to catch up.

Casper and Alex don't even realize I'm here watching them because they're too caught up in screwing to the rhythmic beat of the blaring music that's making the condo's walls vibrate. Still, the music isn't enough to drown out their escalating moans of pleasure.

I want to break out of this hell but I'm mesmerized, watching his hands grip the curve of her hips, his fingertips sinking into her soft flesh, and his muscular arms flexing as they lift her body effortlessly, controlling the speed of their wild and ferocious coupling. Rising up, he takes her breast in his mouth and then drags his tongue along her collarbone, right before their lips connect feverishly.

It's at that moment that I realize that this is more than a mindless fuck session, because Alex never kisses her clients. Ever.

They're together.

At this new understanding, my gut roils as my brain kicks in and attempts to process this. How long has this been going on? Why would the two people I love most do this to me?

But the need for answers is quickly overcome by the surge of intense fury shooting back to my heart, delivering a jolt of electricity, jump-starting it in erratic beats. Now it's exploding with a dangerous concoction of emotions—rejection, sadness, doubt.

And anger. Lots and lots of anger.

As if my body can't take the boiling volatile mixture, my hands begin to shake, my muscles convulse, and finally I erupt, releasing a strangled scream.

CHAPTER 1

Present day

Miniature fingers snap in front of my eyes. "You're glazing over on me, Nic."

Focusing, I scowl as I look down at Hayden. "What nine-year-old calls their mom by their first name?"

"I prefer not to be defined by a number."

"And I prefer to be called Mom."

When I playfully smack the bill of his baseball cap, he crushes my waist with a hug.

"I'll miss you," he says in that sweet voice that never fails to charm me.

I wrap my arms tightly around his bony shoulders and kiss his head, my eyes watering. Part of me has been dreading this day. I don't want to let him go.

"Me too, buddy."

My mother joins our hug, saying, "We'll drop Hayden off at camp Monday," and then leans back to assess my face. "And as for you, try to have fun in Miami."

Mom pushes a strand of my dark hair behind my ear like she did when I was little, but she's obviously holding back what she wants to say. It's easy to read the signs—

watery eyes, red nose, those deep worry lines that bracket her mouth, and the lighter ones that feather out from her tired eyes. She's upset that I'm leaving, though she understands why I must. Thankfully, she won't bring up her concerns with Hayden here.

"This has been your dream since you were little. It's time to make it happen," she says, carrying on the charade and focusing on the positive.

"Mom," I say with a shake of my head, "things changed." I glance quickly at Hayden, tucked against my stepdad's side. George and Hayden are already discussing this week's upcoming meteor shower.

"Interning for Z News is just for the summer," I remind my mom. "I'm twenty-nine, old for this type of position, and the chance that this will evolve into a something permanent is slim."

Even though I'm desperate for the job and the chance to make a better life for Hayden and me, I'm trying to be realistic. The truth is that I'm not sure if I'm capable on many levels.

"Old?" She bats my shoulder playfully as she scoffs at me. "Talk to me in thirty years. Besides, everything happens for a reason, and there's a reason you won this internship over all the other applicants. Give yourself some credit."

She comforts me by rubbing my shoulder and telling me what I need to hear. "There used to be a fire in you, Nicolette," she leans in and whispers. "I know it's still there.

This is your time to fight for what you deserve."

My mother wants the best for me, despite her worrying. It's something I wish she would have done earlier in my life. If she had, maybe I wouldn't have traveled down some of the questionable roads that I did. But if she knew the entire truth about my past, she probably wouldn't let me leave. Ten years ago while she was at home in Alabama, distracted by a nasty divorce from my father, I was at college in Miami and experimenting with very naughty things. A normal mother would have had some inkling that something was amiss, but I suspect that her happy pills kept her blissfully unaware.

It wasn't until I ran home pregnant in the winter of my junior year that Mom began to heal emotionally from the divorce, and we grew closer and put some of our differences aside. I hid myself behind the reserved personality that I'd deliberately nurtured for all these years, trying to be someone she could be proud of. The old me is still there, of course, simmering like molten lava beneath the surface, begging on my weak days to be released. But when it happens, I do my best to lock down that wild spirit, hoping to hide the scandalous truth in my past. I was an assertive person with a prosperous escort business, and I wouldn't take crap from anyone as I pushed my way to the top.

The memories ignite a blazing flame in my chest, energizing me. But just as soon as the thoughts trigger a half smile, I slam the door shut again, worried that the younger, sinful side of me may creep back, showing her true colors to the ones I love.

Having a child quickly changed my priorities, and my life wasn't my own anymore. It's only in these last few years that I decided to brush off an old dream to be an entertainment reporter. At least it's a respectable career—one that I hope my parents and my son can be proud of.

"I'll make the most of it, I promise." Knowing what I need to do, I give my mother the answer she wants, and the one I need to convince myself of.

"That's better." She kisses me on the cheek.

"Mom, I made this for you." Hayden's small hands lift a square box, wrapped with pink paper and a bow.

"Aw, thank you, sweetie." I take it from him and begin to tug on the wrapping.

He places a hand over mine, stopping me. "Open it on your first day of work."

"Okay, I will." I smile and lean in, giving him a year's worth of kisses because I'm desperate for some way to take him with me, but I know it wouldn't work.

"Mom! You're killing me here," Hayden says, his face sour with disgust as he squirms away.

"Don't be so dramatic. Have fun at Space Camp. Make sure you thank Nana and Pop for their *extremely* generous birthday gift." I give them *the look*, the one I often give Mom and George for spoiling him.

"You got a smart kid here, Nicky," George says. "Besides, we promised camp in exchange for one school year of straight As."

"You should know better than to make a bet like that with a brainiac." I pull off Hayden's baseball cap and rub his head where his thick chestnut-brown hair used to hang. Now it's a buzz cut, originally trimmed in this style to hide his hair loss. My heart squeezes in my chest, remembering all that my son has been through these last few years.

I suspect Mom and George knew exactly what they were doing. Not only giving Hayden his dream to act like an astronaut for the summer now that his chemo treatments are finished and his lab and imaging tests are clear, but giving me a summer to finally kick start my career and make a better life for both of us. They just probably hoped I wouldn't choose to return to Miami to do it.

Mom and George stand behind my little nerd, each grabbing his shoulders. I step backward, making my way toward my beat-up red Honda, feeling too guilty to turn my back on him. What mom leaves their child with her parents for the summer to pursue her own dreams?

I wave a trembling hand, my eyes brimming with guilty tears, remembering that I only agreed to take the coveted internship because Hayden was so excited for me. I never expected to actually be chosen. The tedious application process was a long shot, at best.

The night I received the offer e-mail from Z News, Hayden ran around the house screaming that I was going to be on TV. It was a happy moment for both of us. Leukemia made him grow up too soon; he developed a keen understanding of once-in-a-lifetime opportunities, so he refused to let me turn down the chance. At the time, his one-year lab tests had just come back completely clear, so I accepted. Privately I told myself that if anything happened to Hayden in the months leading to the start date, I could always change my mind.

And now that the time has come to actually make the break from my little man, I'm wavering. My hand grips the handle of the car door tightly as I try to reason with myself. Yes, I can see he's healthier, his face full of color and his smile bright. He hasn't been like this in years. He's happy for me, and beyond excited about camp.

I smile and tell myself everything will be okay. If I turn back now it would only disappoint him, and I can't bring myself to do that to him. So I gather my courage, open the creaking driver's side door, and slide onto the ripped seat, shutting it behind me.

Inside, I take a reassuring breath and pull the seat belt over my chest. Then I look over to my sister, Alexandra, relaxing in the passenger seat. Her head's tipped back with her eyes closed, but I can tell she's not sleeping.

"Finally. Could your good-byes take any longer? I think my tits sagged an inch, just waiting for you," she moans.

"I'd say they sagged at least two," I snap back, but quirk my lips into a smile. If I'm going to be stuck with her, I might as well defend myself.

Though she's been visiting more often lately, Alex

never bothers with good-byes, or hellos for that matter. Serious relationships like family scare the shit out of her. With her self-absorbed attitude, I'm probably her only real friend, and after everything we've been through, I'm sometimes unsure why I put up with her crap.

But there's something about having Alex around that gives me comfort. Even though we've had some big bumps along the way, she's one of the few that understands me. And ten years is a long time to hold a grudge against someone you're bound to by blood. At least, that's what I've been trying to convince myself.

"Can you just pretend to be nice and wave?" I plead, hoping to reason with her.

Alex opens one eye and gives me the glare, but then sighs and complies with a fake smile and rolling eyes. I ignore her and wave to everyone huddled in the driveway, then jam the key in the ignition. After a few choked screeching noises, the car reluctantly starts.

With the car rumbling beneath me, I blow kisses to Hayden, whose face is turning red as his eyes begin to glisten. There's an instant tug in my heart to jump out and call the entire thing off, but then he smiles and I remember why I'm risking this adventure. Everything I do is for him. And for that smile alone.

Even as my self-condemnation dries my throat, I press on the gas, turn the front tires out, and pull onto the road before I change my mind completely. I need to remain as courageous as Hayden always seems to be.

Alex, on the other hand, has zero guilt about leaving family. She lights a new cigarette and blows a ring of smoke, stinking up the car while I begin to cry.

"Oh, for fuck's sake, Nic. We aren't even a block away." Alex flips down the torn visor, smiles into the mirror, and rubs at the smear of magenta lipstick on her front teeth with her fingertip.

My sister and I may look alike, we're both tall and thin, have the same long dark hair and fair complexion, but she's a hot, neurotic badass with intense blue eyes. That used to be me too, but now I'm the slightly water-downed version, driven to succeed and keeping my snarky comments to myself. With my sordid past and my Suzy-homemaker present, I'm conflicted about who I should be, even after all these years.

"Sorry, it's not easy for me to be a coldhearted bitch like you."

Alex lifts a shoulder indifferently. "What can I say, I'm a natural."

My sister and I banter; it's what we do. Usually it's in jest, but there's a lot of truth behind our words. It's how we function.

I gesture for her to roll down the window. She does it reluctantly and with a long-suffering groan, but then focuses on her best talent, complaining.

"You're lucky I came to keep you company for a twelve-hour torture ride in this shit box." She smacks her palm on the dashboard, and a cloud of dust swirls into the air.

"I told you that I could have a plane ticket sent to you, like I have before. Remember, I know a Virgin Airways pilot that would do anything for me." She smirks.

"Yes, and what would you do for him?" I counter, though she doesn't need to answer. I have a pretty good idea of what she does for him. After all these years, I think it's still one of her dirty little secrets. "Besides, I need my car for my job. You know, that thing you do to make money?"

"I work!" she says indignantly, throwing her hands in the air as if she's actually offended.

Rolling my eyes, I mutter, "Right."

I know better. After the fall of Angelface, our escort company, Alex started taking the odd modeling job—so she claims, though I'm not sure how. She's been known to lie to make herself look better. But if she's telling the truth, the gigs must be enough to keep her invited to the right parties so she's in the presence of the right people—powerful people who will give her money, cars, jewelry, and apparently plane tickets, just for being their personal eye candy.

Alex flicks a glance my way. "You could have had the same life, you know. We had a good thing going back in college, and you were the one who had to fuck it up by your immaculate conception."

I tighten my grip on the steering wheel, pressing all the blood out of my fingers until my knuckles turn white. "That's not exactly what happened."

My temper rising, I frown at Alex. She conveniently likes to forget the role she played in our company's demise. If she would have stayed away from Casper, maybe things could have been different.

"I mean, don't get me wrong," Alex says, apparently backtracking. "Your little curtain climber's cute and smart, which he obviously gets from me. But he's just so gooey and crusty, or something."

I relax a little, relieved that she's leaving the past alone. I leave it alone too. Locked in a car with her, road tripping for the entire day, is not the time to rehash old grievances. And the truth is, I'm not sure if I even want to go there. I've spent years dwelling over losing our company and Casper, and I really want a fresh start.

It's interesting that she chooses to refocus the conversation on Hayden. Even though she won't admit it, I know Alex has a soft spot for him. Sometimes a backhanded compliment is the best she can do. Or it could be that she's only playing nice because she doesn't want to be abandoned in the middle of the Alabama mud swamp we're driving through to get to the interstate.

"He hasn't been gooey or crusty since he was a baby," I say, correcting her.

"What do you want me to say? I have a paranoia of anything miniature. Animals, kids, donut holes, dicks—I don't discriminate. I don't trust the little bastards. Go big or go home." She waves her cigarette for emphasis, and coiling smoke follows its orange glowing burn.

I let out a little snort. "God, I hope you get your tubes tied."

"I think that's the nicest thing you've ever said to me." Her chin drops on her shoulder and she smiles from over the rim of her designer sunglasses as she pops her shoulders in a perky way.

"You would," I shoot back, shaking my head at her.

Alex sinks back into her seat, getting comfortable for the long haul. We poke at each other through the entirety of Alabama, then she sleeps through northern Florida.

Thank God. The quiet gives me time to think, but most of all, worry. Even though I've landed this amazing internship, I'm terrified that returning to Miami for a prolonged period may churn up old emotions.

Despite the risqué nature of my business in college, I loved my life. I loved the thrill, the money, and the power. And more than anything, I loved the feeling of control.

With Alex by my side as I return to Miami, I'm not sure the fragile outer shell of sugarcoated mommy sweetness that I've cultivated over these past years will withstand the temptations.

My biggest fear is that it will shatter under the pressure.

CHAPTER 2

By the time my car rolls to a dying stop in front of Alex's ritzy, thirty-story modern glass condo building in South Beach, I'm ready to strangle her. But the thing is, she has something I need. She has an extra room in her condo that she bought while we were in college.

I don't dwell on the details of how she manages to pay for it, because the most important part is that it's free, and that's what I need right now. With all of Hayden's medical bills, staying with Alex is the only way I can afford to take a low-paying internship and live in this overpriced, over-Botoxed part of town.

Letting out a sigh, I throw my duffel bag on my new bed before strolling to the window. The view is dark with the dynamic city skyline of Miami behind a row of tall palm trees swaying in the ocean breeze. Just seeing the shimmering lights and energy leaves me wired, knowing that only the salty waters of Biscayne Bay separate me from the excitement.

I take out my phone, snap a photo of the glittering view, and text it to Mom and Hayden, telling them that I arrived. It's too late to speak with them. If I did, I would only break down at hearing Hayden's little voice. I always hate leaving him, but I do on occasion hang out with the whore-beast—a name I've called Alex for years for obvious reasons, one she wears proudly, like an Olympic medal.

At the thought of her, she appears at my door.

"We leave in thirty," she says as she tugs off her clothes.

"To go where?"

"Out." She undresses in front of me, clearly in a rush. The exhibitionist in her never has any shame.

"It's eleven thirty and I've been driving all day. While you slept," I point out, unnerved that I've been here for three minutes and my will is already being tested.

"You owe me for that hideous car ride," Alex says as she hops on one foot, slipping out of the miniscule thong she's wearing. "You know people here don't go out until midnight when the clubs are open until five on the beach and ten in the morning downtown. Besides, I promised to meet someone, and I need you to come with."

Just as I open my mouth to protest, she launches something at my face. The balled-up piece of shimmery fabric smacks my cheek and falls to the floor at my feet. I bend down to pick it up. "What's this?"

"You were about to complain that you don't have anything to wear."

"Actually, I was going to complain that I'm starved and exhausted." I turn the fabric around in my hands, trying to figure out what the hell to do with it. "I'm supposed to wear this? It's a glorified tube top, at best, and I can't even tell if it's for my top or bottom."

"It's for both." Completely naked, she disappears from my bedroom door but shouts back, "Twenty-seven minutes."

There's no sense arguing with Alex. She always wins, or whines until she does, which would honestly be worse than going out. Reluctantly, I give in. It's just dancing. And even though I'm beyond exhausted, I should be allowed to have a little fun while I'm here. I'm not dead, after all.

I take a hot shower that lasts nearly twenty minutes, and then I use the time I have left to dry off, slide into the shiny Band-Aid dress, gather my wet hair into a low slick-backed bun, and dab on a sparkle of makeup.

Alex returns to my room with a pair of booty heels and some chunky geometric jewelry. "Here." She hands everything to me and settles her butt on the vanity, her endless legs stretched out in front of her as I finish primping.

"I don't know why the hell you waste away in those disgusting yoga pants and stained T-shirts. Don't you miss dressing up and living a little?" She kicks at my pile of discarded clothes on the tile floor.

"First of all, those disgusting clothes are comfortable, and there's no chance of wardrobe malfunction like there is here." I gesture to my barely covered double lattes and to the "dress" that ends where my ass meets my legs.

"If you want to be on Z News, you have to look the part.

Get out there and mingle with the powerful rich people, so you can play the media game and glean all their deep, dark secrets," she says sagely.

I let out a sigh because she's right. To be effective at work, I'm going to have to suck it up and pull out a sliver of the old me. A part that would have never given this dress a second thought, or going out at midnight, or getting up after an hour of sleep and working hard the next day.

So I lift my chin, summoning just enough of that person to get through the night, and maybe enough to get me through this summer.

Allowing any more would be dangerous.

CHAPTER 3

Our night begins on Lincoln Road—a pedestrian road in South Beach with bars and restaurants. Tall palms, stories high and wrapped in twinkling white lights, line the walkways. Models, actors, billionaires, and other beautiful people leisurely stroll the avenue, wanting to be seen, and the people sitting at outdoor tables oblige them, watching them eagerly as if it's a parade. This is what Miami's about.

Alex hands me her alligator clutch and stops in front of a darkened retail window. In the reflection, she adjusts her slinky silver dress and lifts her boobs into plump bulbs. When she tweaks her nipples, turning on the high beams, an older man passing by whistles. Another catcalls as she musses her almost-black hair.

"How do I look?" she asks, drawing her red lips into a pout.

"Do you really need to ask?" I smack the purse into her chest, half hoping one boob will deflate.

Jealousy is my sickness, an ugly skin that I can't shed, especially when it comes to Alex. I want to be as carefree and secure as she is. I covet the material life she's somehow held on to when I couldn't, the ease with which she makes money, even though I've achieved nothing since I left college.

I didn't think I needed to. When I ran home, I had a large stash of money. I thought it would last long enough to have Hayden and set our lives on track. But when he became ill, the cost of the pediatric oncologist, hospital stays, and chemo treatments ate through our little nest egg quicker than I could possibly imagine.

Don't get me wrong, I'm not complaining. I would do anything for my child. And the day the account hit zero, I cried, completely sick with inconsolable guilt that I didn't save more so I could take care of him the way he deserves. So since then, I've been the envious spectator in Alex's life for more than one reason. If I had everything she had, Hayden would have only the best doctors and schooling. I would give him anything and everything.

In the past, when I've slipped underwater and drifted into helplessness, I've put my pride and our past aside and asked her for help. Even though there's tension between us, Alex seems to come through for me when it matters most. She doesn't seem to harbor the same love/hate push and pull I have for her.

She functions with very little emotion on the love side, which is why I think she is the way she is. But the small amount she can muster, she gives to Hayden and me. Her affection doesn't appear in the normal way, like with a hug or a smile. Sometimes her good deeds are hidden.

Most recently, her help came in the form of checks. They would appear at just the right time to save me from financial ruin. She's always given me money for Hayden's medical care without question, even though she harbors her own grudge against me—that I left our company to have a child. Her narcissistic mind couldn't and still can't comprehend why I would choose a life without her in my face twenty-four/seven.

"Hold up." She grabs my arm, swinging me back around. "Now it's your turn." Alex slips her hand inside the sleeve of my bolero jacket and pulls, spinning me out of it. I totter like a toy top on the six-inch heels. I wore the jacket thinking I could hide behind it, but I guess that option's gone.

"Where'd you buy this thing?" Alex pinches the fabric between two fingers because she's obviously allergic to anything bought off the rack. "It's garbage." She tosses it in a nearby trash can.

"Hey!"

"Nic!"

She grabs me by the shoulders, preventing me from retrieving it. The twenty dollars I spent on it means nothing to her. I wish it didn't mean so much to me, but every penny does.

"You're going to need to show some skin," she says sternly, "if we're gonna get into that place."

Her gaze drifts to a loud open-air club, pumping music unencumbered into the night sky. Two bouncers with thick necks and tattooed arms guard the entrance to the posh nightclub. No one would probably deny her entrance, but I'm another story. Despite her constant protests about my hotness, next to her bombshell curves and confidence, anyone looks plain. Even me.

For the sake of getting this night over with, I resign myself to the inevitable and allow her to primp me with lipstick, but then she crosses the line and hikes my skirt farther up my thighs.

"Alex, I just pulled that down! My underwear is going to show." I tug the hem south again.

"You wore underwear?" she exclaims.

I give her an incredulous look. Sadly, I know she's not kidding. When she was thirteen and suddenly grew boobs, she stopped wearing undies to church. I'm not sure who was happier, her liberated hooch or the multitude of altar boys who navigated her north and south territories in the confessional.

"Fine. But you better not have on those fucking granny panties."

"I'm not an idiot," I say hotly, but she's already circling me, patting down my ass on a search for elastic lines. Annoyed, I smack her away with a quick whack, but she only laughs.

"Just show a little T and A until we get inside." She inspects me for more adjustments. "Maybe we should have left your hair down?" She stops in front of me, frowning as she peers at my bun.

"I know, I'm hopeless." I look down at myself and

smooth my palms over the silky fabric on my hips, feeling beyond ridiculous. Alex and I are making such a scene that people walking past are looking at me strangely. I may have rocked this look in college, but I was never an escort. My talents were on the business side.

"Shut up, you're gorgeous." She grabs my hand and drags me to the entrance. With Alex, I slink past the bouncers with no problem, skipping the line.

Inside, people pack the club. Some fight their way to the bar while others dance. Wild Latin music reverberates off the walls. The bass is so deep, the music thumps in my chest, vibrating my bones. Women wearing feathers, glittering beads, and high-heeled platforms dance carnival style, elevated above everyone, emitting the local perfume—pheromones, the scent of pure sex.

I weave past several people, heading for the bartender.

"We dance first!" Alex shouts, pulling me a different direction.

"You starve me, shoehorn me into this dress to come out after traveling all day." I yank at the hem, stretching the fabric lower on my legs. "And now, no drinks?"

She doesn't answer, only waves me forward. I groan and follow as we push our way to the dance floor. Couples who actually know how to dance glide around us, spinning, hips gyrating to the rhythm of the salsa music.

I try the same dance moves by myself. I may not ooze the same sex appeal as Alex, but I can definitely hold my own. Years of dancing in the basement when no one was watching was good for something. Several songs later, I have to admit that it feels amazing to let loose for a change, even if it comes at the steep price of a good night's sleep.

In the midst of dancing, I find myself scanning the crowd the way I did when I was in college. I can't help myself; it's automatic. In those days, I was always looking for the hottest guy in the room to flirt with, pluck from the group, and have my way with in a dark corner. Shamefully, that's how I found Casper. Even though I was never an escort, I was uninhibited and oversexed back then, much like Alex. It's a part of me that I've locked away for years, all in an attempt to play my expected role as the perfect mother.

But then an interesting and dangerous thought tickles my mind. For today, away from everyone I know, I can be whoever I want. I grin as I allow the wicked thought to warm me. Before I can stop them, the words grow, twine and wrap within my body, digging roots into my thoughts, leaving tiny hairs pricking the back of my neck with excitement.

I know it's wrong.

My outer shell is already cracking.

I've been so focused on denying myself the things I crave all these years, that I wonder what would happen if I finally gave in? Allowed myself to be the way I want, but only for the summer? Here, trapped in the heat of the swaying bodies of people I've never met, it seems like a plausible idea.

Here, I'm not just Hayden's mom.

Here, I'm simply me.

As soon as I think it, it's too late to pull that thought back. The decision has already been made by my selfish half that often can't be controlled. As a small piece of my protective shell falls away and crashes to the floor, I step onto the remnants and twist the ball of my foot over it, like a discarded cigarette.

Instantly feeling looser, I dig a little deeper into my dance, sliding my hands seductively over my swaying curves in a way that I only would at home when no one was watching. But here, everyone's watching, and for once in a long time, I'm enjoying the attention.

Colored spotlights swirl around in the roiling smoke, highlighting undulating bodies and faces that are smiling and laughing. That's when I spy him. He's perfection—tall, sun-kissed, his features dark and interesting. Light and shadows play on his masculine face as he turns to his friends and smiles with a shit-eating grin. I watch as a dimple punctuates the center of his chin behind a layer of dark scruff.

He turns as if he senses me watching him, and his glimmering gaze finds mine. I stare for a moment, locked in his sights, but as quickly as the connection is made, my play-it-safe warning signals win over, reining in my desire, and I glance away, looking at the floor.

It's been far too long since I played the seduction game. The unexpected moment trips me up, killing the confidence I felt only moments before, and tamps down my uninhibited dancing to an embarrassed gentle bob, making me look more like a parental chaperone for a middle school dance than an exotic dancer.

I turn away from him completely, trying to get my groove back, but my halfhearted attempt is useless because the guy's so attractive. After a few more spins, I find myself peeking in his direction again, praying not to get caught.

If I were eighteen, it would be insta-love and then insta-boom-boom! I zone out for several minutes, lingering on the thought. But I remind myself that even though I'm trying to relax and have fun, I have to be careful not to go too far. Thankfully, Alex saves me by redirecting my attention and shoving a drink in my face, blocking my view of Mr. Hottie.

"Compliments of a friend." She raises her glass to a man with slick dark hair sitting at the bar, a late thirty-something and very handsome. She turns back to me. "Remember rule one, lovely ladies such as ourselves never have to buy our own drinks—ever." She takes a sip of her martini.

"How could I forget?" I smile from behind the rim of my drink and take a sip, feeling that small bit of my past taking over my body, the way it always seems to when I visit Miami to hang out with Alex. And though I'm still testing the current of the water, the rush feels good. With a new shot of liquid courage, I twirl away dancing, and after a few more complimentary drinks by the Mr. Handsome with the dark eyes, whose real name is Marco Cirino, I've loosened up considerably. I may even be on the verge of tipsy.

Alex flirts with Marco, who's charming and obviously wealthy. He's talkative and curious, and when I join them, he asks a lot of questions, seeming very interested in my answers. He's so attentive, I decide that he and Alex are definitely an item of some sort. Client or not, I can't put my finger on it, but he's someone important to her. Someone she trusts.

Several times Alex pulls on his arm, wooing him to dance, but he won't budge. I suspect he's the type who likes to sit back in his ten-thousand-dollar suit and watch. After giving up on Marco, we return to the dance floor, but eventually become separated again in the crowd.

For the time being, I don't care where Alex is. I'm too busy trying to learn the moves to this dance—some interesting new combination of salsa, mambo, and rumba—though most people here are dancing with a partner the way these dances should be. To stay out of everyone's way, I move to the edge of the dance floor, sipping on my newest drink, admiring them. Together they're a throbbing wave of body parts, an enormous dance orgy where every sweaty and sexual movement reacts to another.

Just as I set my empty glass down, a man steps in front of me, blocking my view, and asks, "Would you like to dance?"

CHAPTER 4

As he holds out his large hand in invitation, I catch a glimpse of the man's face in the roaming spotlight. To my embarrassment, I realize he's the same guy that I eye-fucked earlier.

I stiffen, shocked for a moment that he sought me out, but then I smile, painfully aware that despite all the drinks, I'm still feeling conflicted. But mostly because he may somehow know what I'm thinking—*I want to lick you all over.*

With a slight shrug, I say, "I don't really know the moves," offering shyness instead.

"I've been watching you dance, and I doubt you'll have a problem."

His slight Spanish accent is deep, raspy, and beautiful. I'm not sure if it's his voice or the pulsing of the music that's making my insides vibrate. Either way, I'm more than intrigued. My eyes never leave his face, but my mind's roaming the details of his body. Every part. I've been slyly watching him too, taking in his broad shoulders, his lean arms cut with muscle, his slim waist. And the bulge in his pants.

I bite the inside of my cheek. With my reaction, I should be running away but I can't. Up against his good looks, I'm a fluttering moth to a dangerous flickering flame. Maybe I'll have reason to thank Alex for forcing me to come out tonight after all.

He seems so sure of my dance skills, and his smile is so bright against his golden skin, I accept his hand without thinking much past his exotic looks and the lust that I'm internally cursing as he guides me to the dance floor. He faces me and positions my hands, one on his shoulder and one clasped with his.

"These are the basic steps." He steps forward and then rocks back with a cha-cha move. I mirror his lead. We repeat the move successfully only a few times before he pulls me closer, breaking the friendly zone between us. Now pressed against him, I look up but can barely manage a smile because I'm trying to count out the steps.

"Relax!" he says, sensing my awkwardness, and then twirls me away. I don't know how, but he whirls me in a long series of professional spins and twisting limbs, and by the time I'm facing him again, caged within the heat of his lean but strong arms, I'm finally smiling.

"Much better. Get out of your head and feel the music in your hips."

At this advice, each of his strong hands land on my sides, firmly guiding my rolling movements. For a moment, I stop breathing. It's been a really long time since a man touched me, especially one who looks like this.

Without realizing it, I catch myself staring. My face flushes hot with desire, and he seems to smile knowingly, but I convince myself that there's no way he can see the redness of my cheeks under the pulsing lights.

That is, until he leans down and whispers in my ear, "Relax, chica. We're just dancing." With his cheek pressed against mine, his warm breath rushes over my bare shoulder, chest, and back. The blanket of heat it creates urges me to close my eyes, to release my inhibitions and feel my young self again.

I decide to give in to him without question. Under his spell, my heart rate accelerates, pounding with the beats of the conga drum, releasing me into the wildness of it all. I allow his hands to push me wherever they want, to mold my dance movements perfectly with his body.

We rub against each other in sexual gestures. Heat radiates from his wide chest, his abs, his narrow hips, and he spins me so my ass molds to the angles of his pelvis and thighs. His hands splay over my stomach, holding our skimming, swaying, and undulating bodies together in harmony.

With each movement, I'm unraveling, completely simmering in our connection. I tip my head back, resting it on his shoulder, and open my eyes, soaking in the perfection of this moment and how incredibly turned on I am. Taking this as some kind of sign, he raises my arms high above my head and drags his hands sensually down their length along the sensitive skin, over the curve of my waist, and then his hands latch firmly on my hips. He spins me back around, face-to-face, where our lips hover inches apart, out of breath and sucking in the same sweet, sex-filled humid air.

I wanted him when I first saw him, but now I need him. Maybe it's the large quantity of alcohol pumping through my veins, but with his black shirt half unbuttoned and pulled tight over his chest, in combination with that dark brooding face that leaves me unhinged, this could be the sexiest man on earth. A familiar throbbing ache builds between my legs, urging me to seek out the nearest dark corner with my new prize.

I zone out the way I always do when I become turned on. The scenario of what I desperately crave runs through my mind so swiftly that it's merely flashes of quick pornographic images. I can't control myself. I've gone too far too quickly, and everything I've been running from for a decade races to the edge of the cliff like a waterfall. Once the water slips over the side, it plummets, weightless and racing. I just need to enjoy the freefall before the violent crash.

I stop dancing, reach down, and grab his warm hand in mine. With a gentle tug, I lead him through the maze of billowing smoke and dancing couples down the nearest hallway, darkened at the very end.

He doesn't protest. In that primal way, I know he wants me as much as I want him. Even if we don't know each other's names, we know we want the same thing.

Our pheromones give us away; they're raw and animalistic. It's embedded in our DNA and reeks from our breath. Crashing over the edge, leaping into the descent, nothing can stop me.

Taking control, I press him against the wall, not caring who sees. I move my palm over his damp chest, feeling his heart pump wildly beneath, and then run my fingers down the southern path of his buttons until they're roadblocked at his belt. Sitting there they tease, fingertips pacing the horizontal line, dancing along the leather as his eyes follow them. Watching, challenging me, and waiting to see how far I'll go.

Our gaze connects, and he's practically daring me to push further. He has no idea who he's dealing with because I've already lost myself.

Smiling at his challenge, I slip my hand behind the barrier and slide it down into his pants until it connects with his hard-on, and I squeeze firmly. My body's reaction is immediate, and I'm wet just holding him in my hand. Looking up at him seductively, I'm excited for what he has to offer.

He dives in for a kiss as I stroke him. His tongue twists in my mouth as his steamy lips slide in rapid time with mine. I release him when he aggressively lifts me, pulling me closer, as if not to be outdone by our little game. Our bodies grind against each other in a carnal dance, in the same all-consuming fashion as the humidity and wild music that envelop us.

My heart hammers in my rib cage, my body boiling with the need to feel him inside me. Buckles release, zippers loosen, and a condom appears. I hike my knee, locking it around his hip bone, and move my thong to the side to give him easy entry. He grabs my now exposed ass, clutching me tight and hard against him as he drives his thickness inside, filling me.

Together, finally connected, we let out a simultaneous moan. The action is as much of a release as the orgasm, overwhelming, and so long overdue on my end that my eyes roll back into my head with ecstasy. From here on out, he speaks to me not through words but by the commanding way that he takes and owns me. And what he's saying is that he needs this fuck as much as I do.

We climb to the top together, bodies tensing as we rub and bite. From behind, his long fingers slide along the crack of my ass cheek until he's found my wet spot, and with a few mind-altering strokes in coordination with the tremors building inside as he thrusts into me, my pulsing sex explodes with his. We come together in a chorus of moans in the hidden hallway of the club, with the wild music thumping in the background.

One moment we're breathing heavily, clutched to each other in the overwhelming aftermath of the best sex I've had in a decade, and in the next, I blink my glazed eyes and the scenery changes.

The veil of lust lifts and the images are gone. I'm alone in the hallway.

With unsure footing, I wobble backward and hit the wall. The words "I'm drunk" drift through my consciousness, and everything becomes hazy.

Did that just happen? Did I just have sex with someone?

Did I pass out? How long ago?

I spin, looking for Mr. Hottie, only to see a line of girls waiting for the ladies' room down another corridor.

Where did he go?

Steadying myself, I look back down the hallway. The party still continues on the dance floor twenty-five feet away, but he's nowhere to be seen. As I slowly piece together where I am, I make my way down the hall, searching for Alex.

I pull at my clothing, righting it, then slick back my hair and attempt to pull myself together. I step back onto the dance floor just as one song blends into another. People are still dancing as the room tilts and spins like a nauseating amusement ride.

Alex appears right before I stumble and fall, and catches my arm under hers. "You're such a lightweight." She looks between me and someone else. I turn and my gaze finds who—Mr. Hottie. He's with his friends again across the room.

In my confusion, I decide that nothing more than a dance must have transpired between us, only the healthy beginnings of a crazed sexual fantasy in my mind. I must have merely zoned out in a drunken haze on my way to the ladies' room, completely lost in the fantasy world that I knew in college. One where I would take whatever and whoever I wanted, whenever I wanted.

I shake my head, mentally grappling for reality, and reason with myself. I want to believe I'm not that person anymore—that I wouldn't screw a stranger in the middle of a club. I'm a mother now—tame, controlled, safe. I'm not anything like Alex, even though deep down, I long to be exactly the same, despite the fact that there's nothing redeeming about the way she lives her life. It's the darkness in me that's so hard to control.

The hottie is completely unaware that I just dirty-fucked him in my mind, right here in this club with everyone watching. I swallow hard, immediately recalling what I imagined happened, What could easily have happened if I allowed it. And by the look on his face, there's no doubt he would have invited my advances.

Alex is talking but I only hear mumbling. I think she repeats herself when her words break through my alcoholic haze. "Are you ready to go?" She doesn't wait for my answer. Or maybe I did answer because she's tugging me off the dance floor.

"Wait. Hold on." I pull back, unsure if I'm ready to leave. I'm still fighting my overexcited hormones. They're doing a marathon tap dance in my undies.

Alex spins and frowns at me. "Rule number two: Don't get attached to the first piece of hot ass that flexes his dick in your direction."

I cross my arms because it's true, yet I'm undecided how to respond. After a thoughtful moment, I sigh, surmising that it's a good thing she pulled me away. Clearly I was too excited, and it's just a reminder of how easy it would be to fall back into old habits. With Alex's urge to protect me, even in my current state, it seems reasonable that I take things slower from here on out. I let the disagreement go.

"Fine." I blow an annoying loose hair away from my face and stumble slightly in my heels when I cross my arms.

She holds me up. "I saw that look in your eye. I'm on a mission to make sure we have some real fun before you turn into someone's girlfriend, or even worse, a work zombie. You know how obsessive you get!"

"I know." I nod in agreement.

"Good," she says and lifts an eyebrow. "Now can we hit the next stop?"

"And where's that?"

CHAPTER 5

Since Alex is trying to show me a good time, and I'm here to work and not pick up men, I let Mr. Hottie go and dismiss the visions of our dark corner. I follow her to join Marco as he tips the valet who hands him the keys to his car—a silver Aston Martin.

Marco leaves the glittering pastel art deco buildings of South Beach via the MacArthur Causeway, driving toward the neon skyline of Miami. With the salty wind blowing in my face, I'm starting to feel less intoxicated, and thankful that I didn't follow through with my dirty fantasy. I promise myself that I'll maintain control at our next stop.

He takes a quick right and drives across a white bridge. Modern and Spanish-style million-dollar mansions peek between lush tropical vegetation, which wraps the perimeter of Star Island and gives it privacy.

Marco parks on the street and we step out of the car, making our way to a house that is brightly lit and rumbling with loud music. There are bouncers here too, and like a club, you have to either look the part like Alex or be on the exclusive list like Marco to gain entry.

"Do you know whose house this is?" I whisper to Alex.

"Not a clue and don't care." She acts like she belongs, and I try to mimic her. Even if she's annoying and shallow, I want to remember to be completely fearless too. That's the part of her that I admire.

The home is modern with lots of glass, brightly lit from inside. There's a large yard, manicured to perfection and encircled by a high concrete wall. When we step past the bouncers and inside the iron gates, we see an outdoor shower positioned in the side yard. My attention's locked there for several seconds, partly from the shock of seeing more wet flesh than on a European beach, but when my gaze skitters away, it only lands on several outdoor beds adorned with white flowing fabric and a group of people entwined, Kama Sutra style.

"Oh my God." I look to Alex with wide eyes.

"Christ, Nic. Relax."

She misreads me. It's all I can do not to watch them and look like a complete perv. This scene is so far removed from Alabama, yet so familiar from my past, it's a struggle to decide how to respond.

"Maybe we should leave." I start to turn, but Marco gently grabs my arm.

"We'll go out back. Things will be more comfortable for you there," he assures me with an encouraging smile. He's misreading me too. "They're just looking to get noticed. Trying too hard." He waves his hand dismissively at the group, and then tucks a secure arm under mine.

"Well, it's working, I guess." I laugh nervously and give

in because there's an even calmness about Marco, as if he wouldn't judge me, even if I wanted to stop and be a voyeur.

We stroll through the house and out back. An infinity pool lit up with blue lights is the focal point, with the Intracoastal Waterway glistening in the background. Guests arrive via sleek race boats, moored to a nearby dock. Tall palm trees line the property, running like sentinels parallel to a concrete privacy wall.

Here, the party's typical, if one can call extravagance typical. A DJ commands the energy of the undulating crowd, spinning trans beats from a high outdoor balcony. Beautiful people dance and mingle around the pool. The crowd is sophisticated—lots of wealthy men along with lots of younger beautiful women. Alex and Marco fit in perfectly.

We settle on a curved couch underneath a thatched-roof cabana, and a waitress immediately attends to us, taking drink orders.

Marco relaxes in his seat and extends his arm on the back of the sofa. Alex settles next to him, seemingly starting to work on earning her next paycheck, Armani dress, or whatever else her extravagant needs are this week.

"Nicolette, what is it you do for a living?" Marco asks, focusing on me.

"I've just moved here to intern for Z News," I answer, feeling much more in control of myself than while I was at the dance club.

He laughs. "Just promise me you won't be taking any incriminating photos tonight that will land on TV tomorrow."

"You're in luck. I don't start until Monday." I smile as the server returns with our drinks and sets them down on the table, then turn back to Marco. "And what do you do for a living?"

He pauses. "I'm in development." He says the words, but for some reason I don't believe him. Maybe it's the wannabe reporter in me, or more likely it's my bullshit meter from being a mom. Either way, this is the first time all evening that I feel like he's keeping something from me. Otherwise he's been very open.

"Real estate?" I take a sip of my ice water and narrow my eyes.

"*Si.*"

"Any building in particular that I would recognize?"

"Not much, just the entire city." He sweeps his hand through the humid night air, claiming the entire Miami skyline. He seems more confident in his answer than before.

I'm forced to let our conversation go when he stands to greet a woman. With their hands clasped, they kiss each other on both cheeks European style, the way everyone says hello here. Instead of taking the open seat, the woman sits down on the coffee table, facing me.

"And who's this lovely truffle?" she asks in a sophisticated voice as her attention lands on me.

"This is Nicolette Ryan." Marco gestures an introduction. "And this is Caroline Thorn."

"Nice to meet you," I say.

I extend a hand but instead of taking it, she places her hand on my knee and leans in, her gaze roaming as she studies me. I stiffen at her boldness, then drop my hand to my side and sit up straighter, bent on not being intimidated, which seems to be her intention.

As if sensing the tension, Marco continues. "Nicolette just moved here. She'll be interning for Z News this summer."

"Really?" Caroline draws the word out in question, finally releasing me as she leans away.

I relax when she turns her focus to her handbag, sitting in her lap. She unclips the latch, removes her cell phone, taps the screen with her thumb, then lifts the phone, pointing it in my direction. Before I can protest, there's a quick blinding flash.

Shocked, I blink to clear my eyesight. "Did you just take a picture of me?"

As if I didn't even ask the question, she drops her phone back into her purse and gives me a perplexed look. "I feel like I recognize you, or perhaps read your name somewhere. Maybe we've met already?"

Caroline's questions make me more uncomfortable than before. I don't have to see Alex to know she's grinning. She loves it when people are put on the spot, especially when that person is me. Still, I do my best to ignore her and keep an even demeanor.

"No, I don't think so," I lie. The truth is, she could have read about me and remembered if she has a good enough memory. Even though I was never investigated for the crimes of Angelface, which Casper was incarcerated for, many local articles mentioned my name. It doesn't matter how long it's been, it's as though I can never escape my past.

"So, how do you and Marco know each other?" I look between the two, hoping to veer into new conversational territory.

She laughs as if this is the funniest comment in the world. "Everyone who's anyone knows me, love." She reaches back into her handbag as I prepare mentally for another photo shoot, but instead she pulls out a business card. Deftly she flips it over between two fingers, presenting it. I take the card out of politeness, even though it seems she's hitting on me.

"Join us." The s in us lingers like a hiss on her lips. She reaches for my knee again, running her hand seductively over my thigh.

When I tense at her touch, with my response to her invitation lodged securely in my throat, Caroline and Alex laugh at my unease. Somehow I think they would make best friends. Maybe Caroline should be hitting on Alex instead; she might actually get lucky. In fact, I'm sure she would. Though Alex discriminates with size, she doesn't with gender.

The moment is captured on film again, but this time by the quick repetitive flashes of a professional camera being held up from behind a nearby concrete wall of the adjoining backyard. As one, everyone at the party turns to look, only to see several security men dressed in black rush to jump the barrier and tackle the hidden paparazzi. The muffled sounds of a scuffle drift to us over the wall.

"I guess that's my cue to leave." Caroline rocks forward and stands, smoothing her dress. "*Ciao*, Marco." Her gaze slides over Alex, ignoring her, and swings back to me. "*Ciao, bella.*"

She turns to leave, and I can't help staring at her slim and regal body. Her scarlet sheath dress slides over her lean curves as she moves through the crowd. Everyone parts from her path as if she's royalty, or was it Moses? She must be someone important for the paparazzi to track her down for photos.

Join us. I replay her words in my head, but in light of her flirtatiousness, I'm not sure I want to know what she means. I look down at the business card, but all I manage to see is a streak of black because Alex snags it from my fingers before I can read anything.

"You need to stay away from that," she warns, shoving the card into the bra cup of her dress. I have a feeling that she's not just talking about Caroline Thorn.

"What did she mean? Join who?" I gesture toward Caroline, who's now boarding a luxurious boat that's docked nearby.

Alex leans close and whispers to me the way she always does. "I've only heard rumors. It's a very exclusive underground group, and trust me, with your new squeaky-clean life, you'll want no part of it."

CHAPTER 6

Alex refuses to tell me more about the questionable group that Caroline Thorn invited me to, but she seems to know much more than she's letting on. The mystery intrigues me but for now, I let it go.

At Alex's insistence and to my chagrin, especially after the fiasco of Friday night, we party nonstop all weekend. I only pause to chat with Hayden over the phone each day. It's amazing how much I can miss him, and I've only been gone for a short period of time. He's in better spirits than when I left, though, which helps me fight off my own heartbreak that only relents when we chat.

Feeling a little sorry for myself, I drag myself onto a lounge chair by the condo's pool and collapse in a restless nap. In my dreams, Alex flirts with every man at the pool, and when I wake up, I'm positive it really happened because every one of them watches with salivating gazes as we leave.

• • •

Monday rolls around entirely too fast, leaving me exhausted for the first day of work. I report bright and early at eight thirty a.m. to the station's office on the fortieth floor of one of the tallest buildings in downtown Miami.

When the elevator doors open, a bright white modern lobby greets me. A receptionist sits behind a long, sleek desk with the Z News logo emblazoned on the wall behind it. I stride to her and she lifts a single finger in the air, signaling that she'll be with me momentarily. After wrangling a symphony of rings and transferring several phone calls on her switchboard, she finally returns her attention to me.

"How can I help you this morning?" Her smile is impossibly large—and very fake in every sense of the word. Botox. Caps.

Snob.

"I'm the new intern. My name is Nicolette Ryan." A single drop of nervous sweat rolls down the middle of my back. I can't believe that I'm actually here, after all this time.

"Oh, welcome. If you would just take a seat with the other interns, someone will be right with you." She gestures to a grouping of white leather chairs where two other people are seated, both looking as nervous as I feel.

"Thank you." I nod and shuffle to them in my heels and take a seat.

"Hi!" I extend my hand. "I'm Nic."

The girl, blond and perky, perhaps twenty or so, reaches for my grasp first. "I'm Casey. Are you our new boss?"

"Nope, I'm an intern too."

"Oh, sorry. I just figured you were somebody since

you're old." Despite her words, I sense no remorse in her expression. In fact, she's smiling.

I sit up straight and narrow my gaze, doing my best to control my expression and the jittery hand clenching the strap of my handbag that wants to retract and smack her upside the head. Instead, I rein in my reaction and turn my attention to the boy sitting next to her.

"Nic." I reach out a hand in greeting.

"Jackson." His umber-brown hand connects with mine. He's young too, with thick black glasses and perfect hair, wearing a bow tie and a plaid shirt beneath a trendy hipster heather-gray sport coat.

"Don't mind Casey. I've been here for exactly five minutes, and I can already tell she's a frigid, jealous bitch."

Casey gasps.

Jackson already has my heart, but I bite my lip to conceal my urge to smile. To keep everyone relaxed, I do my best to rally in a mature, motherly fashion. "There's room for all of us. We were all lucky enough to get the job, right?" It seems I need to defuse the catfight that's about to start, and I've only been here for two minutes.

"Actually, there will only be room for one," interrupts the man who walks up and stands before us.

We all look up in his direction.

"I'm Vega Luna. It's nice to meet you." His gaze sweeps from Casey to Jackson as they introduce themselves, and then stops on me. He smiles with the same shit-eating grin he had on Friday night when he molested me on the dance floor and I loved every fucking second.

Holy Jesus, Mary, and mother of all hotties, the mystery man I seduced in my mind is my new boss.

At the realization, time nearly stops. My heartbeat pounds in my ears until I'm sure the color on my face seeps away, leaving me chilled in the most awkward situation I have ever experienced. I can't even hide behind a smile like I did with Casey's crappy comment because I'm completely and utterly mortified.

But the largest and most concerning problem is that now that I see him up close, I realize that I know exactly what it's like to taste that sexy skin of his. In fact, I'm pretty sure that I didn't just screw him in my mind like I believed for the last several days, but that I screwed him in real life.

I really did have sex with Mr. Hottie.

And he's my boss.

Oh. God.

"Nice to see you again," he says, his accented words rolling off his lips like honey.

He reaches out, his gaze intent on mine, and when I accept his warm hand, I'm jolted with the same sexual attraction that ran through me the other night when we danced. It leaves me so weak in the knees that I feel them giving out beneath me. Just as he releases his grip, I reach for the nearest chair to hold myself upright.

"You too," I say in a small cracked voice that I barely recognize as my own, then drop my gaze to the floor, trying not to pass out from shock.

Unable to control where I look, my attention flicks back to Vega. As he chats with Jackson and Casey, I take time to digest this work version of him.

He looks as delicious as he did on Friday night, but today his hair hangs loose in dark waves that frame his face. A long leather cord drapes around his neck and falls into his white dress shirt. Even with the top button open, his shirt fits snugly across his chest beneath a camel-colored sport coat, the color of which accentuates his honey-flecked brown eyes. With his worn-in jeans, he's the picture of sexiness—confident, slightly unkempt in a manly way, and smoldering. Now that I can see him clearly in the daylight, sans alcohol, I take in that he's a few years too young for me, and my boss.

Just kill me now.

"Follow me and I'll explain how this summer internship's going to play out." He beckons for us to follow.

I drift to the back of the group, cursing Alex for forcing me to go out Friday. If we hadn't, I would have never met Vega in that context. Or should I call him Mr. Luna? I roll my eyes at the thought.

Trying to muster my courage, I follow them through the glass door that separates the lobby from the bustling activity of the newsroom. Cubicles extend in rows down the length the large space, each containing a desk stacked high with papers. Employees scurry down aisles between the rows, answer phones, and hunch over computer keyboards, tapping out e-mails. TVs mounted to the walls show other channels reporting the news. At the far end of the newsroom is an anchor desk set against floor-to-ceiling windows that showcase a backdrop of the teal-colored tropical waters of Miami Beach. Multiple video cameras point toward two beautiful anchor people, taping today's entertainment news.

Despite feeling humiliated, I halt for a moment to take in the scene—the bright lights, the anchors, the camera-men, and the producers. They're all here, just like I imagined. Finally seeing it in person reads like a daydream. Everything that I've worked for these last few years, career-wise, is within my reach.

I take a deep breath of satisfaction before realizing the group has left me behind. Embarrassed, I rush to catch up with them as they funnel into a conference room. Vega holds the door open for us and as I pass, I do my best to ignore him, holding up my chin and looking straight ahead.

"Take a seat," he says, and allows the glass door to swing shut.

When the interns are settled around a conference table, Vega stands at the front of the room. "Welcome to Z News. As you know, my coworker Tandy hired you, but since then she's been promoted to a new position, so you'll be working with me. I hear that you're the top three of over two hundred candidates. So, congratulations on making it this far," he says, glancing at each of us in turn.

"What did you mean when you said that there would

only be room for one of us?" Casey says, interrupting him. I sit up a little straighter, anticipating his response, since I'm a little worried about that statement myself.

"Right." Vega adjusts his stance. "Usually, all interns are offered some kind of position if they can hack the long hours and high pressure—if they make it, which is rare. However, this year there's only one spot available for a full-time junior producer, a spot I hope will be filled by one of you."

His gaze flickers to me, and the nervous chill that I was feeling melts away and is quickly replaced with the same heat that rolled between us Friday night. I press my lips together to hide the smile tugging at them and drop my gaze, hoping he can't see my cheeks flame.

Get it together! Are you going to fizzle every time this guy looks at you? I suck in a deep breath as I roll back my shoulders and tip my head upward, then set my jaw, determined to get my shit together. I'm a professional and an adult—who just happened to have casual sex with another adult.

When I focus back at the group, Casey and Jackson are eyeing each other like opposing contestants on a reality show, and then they turn to assess me. This internship has become more than a job, it's become a competition where the weakest person will sink and the strongest will rise, commanding a real job.

This news is as exciting as it is nauseating. I have a chance to attain my dream job, one that would provide security for Hayden and me. And maybe it would eventually mean a new car, and a house for just the two of us. From here, the sky could be the limit. That is, if I can beat out these two for the opportunity.

"If all three of you survive," Vega continues, "the final decision will be based on who uncovers the best news story, which is due the last week of the internship. Whoever's chosen will deliver their findings on the air at the end of the summer."

"On camera, in front of the whole world?" Casey asks, nearly bobbing out of her seat with excitement.

"Yes, but that's just one of your responsibilities. You'll also be in charge of writing posts and updating social network outlets such as Twitter, Instagram, Tumblr, Facebook, and our blog. You'll assist me with story research, help at events, answer fan mail, and make it your goal in life to learn the names, bios, and dirty laundry of every celebrity, politician, business mogul, and philanthropist."

At that, Vega leans onto the table with both strong arms. "With the gossipy nature of our show, you must know who's important before they become important. Who's fucking before they fuck. Sometimes these things occur within a matter of hours—or minutes."

Or seconds.

My body temperature increases, remembering it took him exactly three seconds to pull me under his sex-induced spell. He grins at me as Casey and Jackson laugh, completely unaware that Vega and I dirty-rubbed all over each other three days ago. I can't help but smile back this time. It seems it's just one of the things he has the ability to seduce out of me.

"The bottom line is that you'll only survive in this business if you're informed and able to react quickly," he adds. This makes me think back to Caroline Thorn at the party on Friday night, and how I had no idea who the hell she was, even though everyone else did. It's a big red flag waving around, warning me how unprepared I am.

Yes, I've spent many years finishing college in night classes, studying during the long hours of Hayden's chemo or after he went to bed at night, preparing for this job. But apparently it wasn't enough. Unlike me, Jackson and Casey aren't freaking at the list of responsibilities, they're giddy with excitement because they probably know social networking platforms inside and out, and breathe the stink of every higher roller ever mentioned on Z's blog.

I'm in serious trouble.

"I'll show you around the office, get you settled at your desks, and checked in with HR. Any questions?"

We shake our heads.

"Then let's go." He opens the door and holds it again, waiting for us to pass through. Casey and Jackson exit first, but when I attempt to slink past again without making eye contact, he says, "Nicolette," and lightly touches my arm.

"Yes." I pause and look up.

Vega waits for the others to move out of earshot before

speaking. "About Friday night, I'm so sorry. I had no idea who you were. I didn't even know I would be your boss until this morning."

"How could you?" I say with a shrug. "I never introduced myself, and I only interviewed with Tandy."

"Still, it's against Z's work policy to fraternize—"

Even though I gave in to my desires this past weekend while partying, I'm in Miami for this job. My goal is to build a better life for Hayden, and I won't let anything get in the way. So I give him a brittle smile and cut him off. "What was it you said to me at the club? 'Relax, *chica*, we're just dancing.'"

"Right, just a dance." His lips twist into what seems to be his signature smartass grin.

Vega doesn't have to say anything more for me to know what he's thinking. I can't deny that our salsa dance was hot sex on a stick. Rules or not, if I had the chance to let his strong hands roam my body again, pressing us together, trapping the heat between us, I would have a difficult time saying no.

And by the look on his face, he most definitely would too.

CHAPTER 7

"I'm fucked."

"So your first day went well?" Alex joins me on the balcony of her condo where I'm practically inhaling a fruity Argentine Malbec straight from the bottle.

"Remember that guy I danced with on Friday?"

"How could I forget," she says dryly.

"Turns out that I'm pretty sure I screwed him in the hallway at the club—and he's my boss."

"Are you serious?" Her eyes widen with delight. When I nod, she belts out a laugh. "I guess I should have separated you two earlier."

"Tell me about it." I take another gulp of wine.

"Your poor starved and shriveled vagina was probably clutching like a grabby hand, hungry for a meal. I'll bet you devoured him like a sex buffet."

I purse my lips, withholding my response. Her assessment is truer than I would care to admit. Alex has a way of saying things that I only internalize.

The truth is that I've been trying to piece together the sexual encounter with Vega all day. As I stealthily watched him in the office, memories of his anatomy became distinctly clearer. The thing is, fantasies don't have the de-tails that I remember. The weight of him against me, the fullness of his lips devouring mine, the way his fingers claimed me and pressed into my skin, and his smell—leather and spices. I couldn't have imagined that scent if I tried. Anything that delicious would have been beyond my realm of imagination. All the images that I manage to retrieve sprint through my mind in a collage that leaves me staring into space.

I shake my head, trying to hold on to what's real and continue my rant. Sometimes that's hard for me when my mind starts to wander.

"On top of that, it turns out the internship is a contest between me and two other interns to find the best story by the end of the summer. Whoever wins gets the real job. And my competition is young, energetic, and driven."

"And what the hell are you?" She sips her dirty martini and props her bare feet up on the glass railing.

"Old, wrinkled dead meat."

"You need my help? You know I can sabotage those little bitches." She traps an olive between her teeth and snaps them shut, beheading the spear like a guillotine in a gruesome demonstration of how she would "help."

"Can you? That would be nice," I joke and take anoth-er sip of my wine, happy to have someone see my side of things.

"You know I hate anyone younger than me," she says.

"You hate everyone."

"At least I own it. You feel the same way, you just won't admit it."

We're more similar than I care to acknowledge. Alex is me if I acted how the hell I wanted, and that is and always has been the root of my jealousy.

"Alex, you know what I need." I shift in my seat until I'm facing her so I can give her my most persuasive puppy-dog eyes, unsure if she'll give me what I want. "I need for you to tell me about that club Caroline Thorn invited me to. That may be my ticket to my dream job. I can write circles around those two twits and win this. If I can get in there and see what the secret group is about, there's a story there."

"For once, can you listen to me?" Alex places her martini on the table and leans on the arm of my chair. "You need to leave that shit alone. Trust me." Her eyes are sharp and serious. She rarely does anything nice for anyone, but she does look out for me when it really matters. It may be on her very short list of redeeming qualities.

I tip back the bottle, finishing the last drops of wine as I consider her reaction. Whatever information she's hiding must be primo, otherwise she would relent.

Done, I set the bottle on the small table next to my chair. "You know I can't do that." When I decide on something, nothing stops me until I get what I want.

"You're so stubborn!" She abruptly stands, picks up her empty glass, and storms inside the condo through the open sliding glass doors. It's not very often I can get under her skin, but we do have the same genes, after all.

"You know I'll find out some way. It'll just be easier if you help me." I jump up and follow her inside, trying to reason with her.

Alex glances over her shoulder, clenching her jaw as she shoots a cynical glance my way, but otherwise she ignores me, continuing to the kitchen to make another drink. As she removes the jar of olives from the fridge and the vodka bottle from the freezer, I pass by, making a bee-line for her bedroom. If she's not going to help me, I'll help myself. I really need that business card, and I'm positive it's here somewhere.

"What the hell are you doing?" Her feet pad across the tile floor as she follows me. At the same time, we launch forward, making a run for her bedroom, and collide shoulder to shoulder with flailing limbs like children. I grapple with her, holding her back with my hand as I duck into her room, slamming the door in her pissed-off face.

"Nic, goddammit, get out of my room!" she yells, her voice muffled on the other side.

She jiggles the knob and bangs on the door, but I've already locked it. My heart races the way it always does when we fight; there's always been a healthy sense of competition between us, which usually ends in disaster.

When I turn, I cringe at the explosion of disorganized shit she calls a boudoir. She's always been messy, but this is a junkyard of old pizza boxes, empty Absolute bottles, and pill bottles, with dirty clothes strewn everywhere.

Scanning the room, I see no sign of the clothing she wore on Friday night, so I bypass everything and head for the dirty laundry in her walk-in closet. There, I quickly search through each piece of clothing, but the longer I take, the louder and angrier Alex becomes. Her banging and screaming become frantic.

When I find the dress she wore that night, I hold it up, look inside, and shake it, hoping that the card will fall free. But it's not here, so that means she actually put it somewhere on purpose.

Just as I race across the room, I pause and note a new noise. She's shoved something in the doorknob, making metal click against metal, like she's trying to jimmy the lock. With her new approach, I only have a few seconds left, so I rush to her jewelry box. As teenagers it was her favorite place to keep important items. I riffle through the compartments and sift around the jewelry, but still find nothing.

Out of ideas, I let out a little growl of frustration.

The lock clicks, the knob turns, and the door creaks open. On the other side, Alex appears stone-faced and psychotic, like she's ready to kill me. "You're not going to find it. I burned it with my lighter."

My bullshit meter dings. "You're such a liar. If you did, you wouldn't have tried to keep me out."

She takes two steps forward and I step back two, only to stumble over a pile of heels and lose my balance, tumbling to the floor. Alex laughs, but this time she shouldn't because with my new vantage point from the floor, I think I just found her secret hiding place.

I leap to grab the business card hidden on the underside of the lampshade on her dresser. Just as I snatch the card, Alex charges and tackles me the way we fought when we were young, and we fall entwined onto the bed.

"Give me that!" She jabs me in the face with her elbow and smacks my arms, scrambling for the tiny piece of paper. I twine my fingers in her hair and pull, ripping out strands by the root, making her screech like a banshee.

"Get off, you crazy bitch!" I break away and scramble off the mattress to stand in a defensive crouch, breathing heavily. "I don't understand what the big deal is!" I wave the card at her. "What the hell is this all about? You never give two shits about anything!"

"Fine, you got your stupid card, but don't ever tell me I didn't try to stop you."

I take it as a warning that I should pay attention to, but I need this story, because I need this job. And no matter what Alex says, she won't stop me. She pulls herself to a sitting position, trying to calm her heavy breathing while brushing her tangled hair away from her face with her fingers. "You'll never figure out what it means, anyway."

I look down at the card, flipping it from side to side as I realize that it's completely blank on both sides.

CHAPTER 8

The business card is taped to the bottom edge of the monitor of my computer at work. For the last three days, I've been trying to figure out how to read the damn thing. But as far as I can see—in any light, under heat, in cold, and in every experiment I've tried Inspector Gadget style—it still says nothing.

Taking a break from writing a blog post for Z, I research Caroline Thorn, looking for any clues to what this secret group is about, but there's nothing. She's a widowed philanthropist with billions of dollars who rescues puppies and feeds the world's hungry—literally. She dines with state and church dignitaries to further her causes, all noble and nothing secret. On paper she's a saint, which makes the possibility of outing whatever this thing she's a part of even more enticing.

I take a deep chug of black coffee to recharge. As I do, everyone in the news office laughs just like they've been doing all week.

"What the hell is with everyone?" I slam the mug to the desk. I'm exhausted from working long hours, from restless sleep, and from dealing with Alex.

My gaze jumps from Casey to Jackson, who are covering their smiles with their hands, and then to other members of the office, who desperately try to keep their gaze on their computer while wrangling a knowing smile.

No one answers.

This has been going on all week. Every day. Several times a day.

From my desk I can see everyone over the low cubicle walls. They told me the lack of privacy is to encourage discussion among team members, but I've only noticed it as a way for everyone to be in my business and torture me.

"Nic!"

When the raspy voice I love calls to me from across the room, my tense body jumps slightly and then relaxes at the soothing sound. I look over and find Vega on the phone, waving for me to come to his office.

I clear my throat and stand, dismissing everyone, and smooth down my pencil skirt before making my way to him. Once I reach his door, he gestures for me to enter and sit, and I do as he finishes his call. After he drops the phone on the base, he leans forward, elbows propped beneath him, his handsome face serious and intent on mine.

"Nic, are you enjoying your coffee?"

"My coffee?"

"I see you drink a lot."

"I've been working a ton of late hours, and need the caffeine. Is there a rule against that?" I snap, still annoyed with everyone in the newsroom.

"Of course not," he says mildly, "but you should probably check the bottom of your mug."

"What?"

My eyebrows lift in shock, and I grasp the chair's arms to hurl upward and rush out of his office. With determination, I speed around the maze of cubicles back to my desk. There I lift my mug in the air and peer underneath, only to find a piece of paper glued to the bottom. In bold block letters it reads BICTH JUICE.

Oh. My. God.

Everyone laughs openly this time, probably because they realize what's been happening all week is playing in my mind. For each of the ten cups of coffee I sucked down a day, every time I took a sip from the mug, my colleagues saw the words "bitch juice."

Motherfuckers.

Though humiliated, I stiffen my posture and rally with my best Alex comeback. "Watch your back, girls."

Her words slip from my mouth so easily in the instances when I have to defend myself. I launch dagger eyes at Casey and Jackson, grab my mug, and head for the office kitchen to tend to my wounded pride.

When I stomp in the room, I'm pissed beyond belief. Everyone who's lingering in the break room must see my expression because they quickly gather their things and jet. When they're gone, I shut the door, hoping to sever myself from the disaster of my first week, and it's only Thursday.

Angry, I move to the sink, toss the remainder of the coffee, then turn on the hot water, letting it rush over the bottom of the cup. My thumb slides over the photo of Hayden and me printed on the side. Beneath the photo it reads WORLD'S BEST MOM, but maybe it should say WORLD'S STUPIDEST MOM. The mug was Hayden's gift to me before I left home, the one I promised to open on my first day of work. A cherished present from my little guy, but now it's ruined.

My eyes blur until plump, hot tears slide over the rim and trickle over my cheek. I miss Hayden so much, and I wonder if I made a massive mistake moving here. For some reason my peers have singled me out, making this even harder. Maybe because I'm the different one, the mom turned working woman.

I hate that they're getting to me. Why isn't being friendly and hardworking while doing a good job enough?

The door creaks open, but I don't bother looking. It could be Casey or Jackson coming to finish me off with whatever practical joke they have planned next. The sad thing is, I have a good sense of humor, and I can usually take it as well as dish it out. I'm an expert because of my relationship with Alex, but only if the motives aren't meant to be hurtful, which isn't the case here, at least where it involves Casey.

Whoever has joined me shuts the door and steps forward until they're standing right behind me. The air pressure in the room changes, and without looking, I know it's Vega. Not only does his intoxicating spicy cologne give him away, but also the way the hair on my neck prickles whenever he's near.

"I'll discipline them for office hazing if you want," he says, his voice comforting but firm. "But I think that will only make things worse."

In response, I shake my head, still focusing on digging my fingernail into the paper on the bottom of the mug. Under the warm stream of water, tiny rolls of paper peel away little bits at a time and drop into a pile within the stainless steel sink.

"I know this is a tough transition for you, but I've read your résumé, your story samples, and watched your audition tapes, and you should know that I think you're really talented. Enough to blow those two shits out of the water."

A pop of a laugh escapes despite my runny nose. "Then what am I doing wrong?" I turn off the water and dry my hands with a paper towel, giving up on the mug for now. "You're too good and they see it. They're jealous."

I spin and lean against the counter. "You're joking, right?"

Vega gives me a sad look, and I'm immediately aware of the way I must appear to him. I wipe my damp face with my palms. "Sorry, you must think I'm a wimp."

"No, well—yes."

He laughs and his honesty makes me laugh.

"Thanks," I say with a wry smile.

"What I mean is, you just need to toughen up and grow

a titanium skin. You're extremely talented, but you'll never survive in this business if you don't. It's vicious and competitive, and there are colleagues everywhere just waiting to be nice to your face and then stab you in the back."

"How do I know you're not one of them?" I don't know why I take the chance and ask, but I do. My thoughts seem to spill out so easily around him.

Vega drops his chin to his chest, and his hair falls into his face as he chuckles. "You're just going to have to trust me, I guess."

"That's the problem, I already do," I whisper, and clench the squared edge of the linoleum counter as I say the forbidden words.

Despite what happened between us in the club, we've been on our best behavior, skirting around each other all week, avoiding eye contact, and trying not to chat for longer than necessary or about anything but work. But still, it's hard to deny that there's a spark of something between us, even if something so small is prohibited by work rules. "I think I trust you too." With his hands deep in his pockets, he glances at me from under his long dark lashes and smiles with that panty-dropping grin.

With those words, even though it's wrong to feel something for him, he's just turned my day around.

"It'll get better," he promises, and moves closer to place a hand gently on my shoulder.

Without counting, I already know it's been three days, three hours, and thirty-two minutes since he last touched me on the same spot. The last time was on my first day of work.

"Thanks for the advice."

Our gazes lock for longer than appropriate as each of us stands there, wearing a dumb smile. The intensity of our attraction becomes too much to bear, and one of us must break away.

Finally he nods and drops his hand, digging it back into his pocket. But he stands immobile, as if he's trying to decide if we should say any more. We probably shouldn't.

Vega must think the same because he turns away. I watch him walk away, savoring the view. His jeans hang low over his narrow hips, accentuating the hard curves of his perfect ass. If there were a dark corner at work, he'd really be in trouble.

When he leaves and shuts the door, I drop into the nearest chair and begin laughing hysterically. Maybe I'm just stressed out. Or maybe I'm so amped up with caffeine, anger, fear, and confusion about who I should be—and let's not forget the horniness—that I just need to let it all out. As I do, coworkers striding past the glass walls give me a strange look.

Screw them. Let them think I'm batshit crazy if it will keep them out of my way.

I take my phone from my pocket and text Alex.

Drinks at Smith's @ 5:30?

CHAPTER 9

Marco and Alex are sitting at the bar when I arrive at Smith's. I drop my handbag on the countertop and pull up a stool next to them.

"Hey, Marco."

"Nicolette, how lovely to see you." He gives me a kiss on each cheek, but looks surprised. "I wasn't expecting you."

"I thought a drink would be good after the day I've had. You been here long?" I look at my watch. It's already seven, much later than I promised to meet Alex. I hate that time always slips away without me realizing.

"I've been here since about five thirty, but sorry that I can't stay longer. I was just about to leave. In fact, I'm late for a meeting."

"Oh no." I act sad, but I'm actually relieved. Even though he's friendly enough, there's something off about him.

Marco leans in and plants a kiss on my cheek. "*Ciao, bella.*"

We wave as he leaves.

"'Ello, love," Alex says.

She's forgiven me for ransacking her room and stealing the business card. Partly because she thinks I may never figure out how to read it, and partly because I depleted my small stash of cash to buy her a bottle of her favorite and very expensive vodka.

If I had more money, I could probably buy the information I need. Lord knows I have tons to blackmail Alex with, though the truth is that attention whores are impervious to blackmail. She would only revel in any publicity the leaked information gave her.

"Sorry I'm late." I shift my weight on the stool of the outdoor bar. On the waterway behind us, a cruise ship sails past, leaving for the week. When its horn blows, everyone at the bar erupts in a cheer and wave to the people on deck.

"How was work?"

She knows it's going shitty, so I deflect. "I should ask you the same."

"Touché." She sips her drink, avoiding the fact that she's done absolutely no work since I arrived, at least that I'm aware of. "I love it when you're feisty with me." She pats me on the back like a proud mother. When I stand up to her, it's the only time I have her respect. I think it may be the only time I have my own respect.

"Any luck with your little project?" She waves a finger in my face.

I blow out a long sigh. "Are you sure there's no way I can barter for the info?" I take out the blank card from my purse and set it on the counter between us, hoping there's some way I can make her feel sorry for me, though it's a lost cause. If she thinks she's trying to protect me, she won't budge.

"With what?" She laughs. "You have no money, and you know I don't want your kid. The only thing that ancient car is good for is scrap metal."

I look away, deflated.

"You're assuming I can," she mumbles.

"What's that?"

She bobbles her head and rolls her eyes, then sips her martini.

"Meaning you can't because then you'd have to kill me, or something?"

She takes a drag off her cigarette and focuses her gaze on me, then turns her head to blow smoke in another direction.

It's up to me to guess. So I do.

"You're a part of it?" My eyes widen. I should have known. She knows everything, not just idle gossip.

"Nic, please. You're making my head spin with all the questions."

"That's the alcohol, Alex!" I say a little too loudly. Everyone around us is watching us banter, but I'm used to it because it happens frequently.

She slides off her stool, looking tipsy and it's still early, even for her. She grabs her Hermès handbag and leans into me. As she does, she stumbles into the counter, causing her purse to nudge a martini glass. It topples over and the contents spill across the bar, submerging the business card.

"Oh, shit. Sorry," she says, but her face doesn't match her words. She simply smiles and disappears. As usual, Alex is doing her best to sabotage all hope.

"Crap!" I pick up the card, now half-soaked and ruined as it drips with a vodka mixture.

I hold up the card to dry it off with a napkin, and that's when the dying sunlight catches the card at a certain angle. For a split second I see a flash of a letter, just one beautiful letter. I lean in to look closer, unsure if my eyes are playing tricks on me.

CHAPTER 10

Against my better judgment, I'm standing in the dark in the middle of the deserted Miami warehouse district near the airport. Grimy windows are shattered. Rats scurry among the garbage, and my car is parked a block away. My pepper spray is gripped securely in my hand, loaded and ready if needed.

Turns out that I only needed to submerge the business card in liquid to read the contents. Then as fast as I read it, the paper disintegrated in my hand, turning to mush on the wood bar top at Smith's. But before it did, the card requested one thing—that I be standing at this desolate location at exactly ten thirty p.m.

The sound of heels tapping over the gravel, splashing in puddles from a recent thunderstorm, steals my attention. Feeling edgy, I flip the lid of my spray and place my finger on the pump button, standing ready for anything. A woman's silhouette appears from a nearby alley, strutting in my direction. When her face reaches the beam of the streetlight, I recognize her.

"Raine Whitezman?" I relax the grip on my weapon.

"Who are you?" She stands several feet away, looking as

guarded as I feel. We have never met, but I've seen her anchor the local news. Her long platinum locks and striking angular features are unmistakable.

"Are you here because of a disappearing card?" Ignoring her question, I don't give her my name. I'm unsure if I want anyone to tie me to this secret group.

"Took me forever to figure out how to read it. Not sure why the person that gave it to me just didn't tell me what it said in the first place."

I've already thought about this myself. "They wanted you to be invested. They wanted you to want to know."

"Well, it worked. I've been obsessing over it for a week. Any idea what it's about?"

Unlike me, she doesn't seem to have a clue. If I didn't have Alex, I probably wouldn't either. "No," I lie. If this ends up being some sort of story, I want it to be mine and mine alone. I can't allow her to scoop me with the biggest story of the year—I hope.

"Right." She inspects me from head to toe. She has her own bullshit meter, and I'm sure it's waving red flags.

A car appears in the distance. Its headlights bob with the uneven back road riddled with potholes. Raine and I step closer to each other. Even if we aren't acquainted, it's clear we're in this together. A black Rolls Royce limo stops in front of us, and I look at her uncertainly.

The driver steps out and opens the back door. "Ladies, please." He waves us in.

"So are you going to tell us where we're going?" I ask him.

He only shakes his head. With one look at his stone-faced facade, it's apparent that he's not going to give up any information. Under normal circumstances, I would be running the other way, but this is too strange and curious for me to back out now. My bright future depends on it, and the wannabe reporter in me can't help herself.

Despite the possible danger, I step into the back first and slide across the creamy leather seat. Raine follows and settles facing me. Just as quickly as the door shuts, the locks snap, holding us prisoner. Raine jumps, skittish at the sound, and I'm wishing I had something other than pepper spray, which is useless trapped inside this car.

When the car drives off, black metal sleeves slide over the windows, blocking us from the passing scenery and rendering our compartment nearly black.

"This is making me nervous," she says, her shaky voice cutting through the darkness. With her reaction and the secrecy around this entire scenario, I'm starting to have second thoughts. I'm about to bang on the divider to alert the driver to let me out when something captures my attention.

"What's that?" I ask.

A noise sounds, electronic in nature. More sliding. Then an image appears on a small dual-sided flat-screen TV that's rising from a hidden compartment on a small tabletop that separates us.

An image appears on the TV, filling the compartment with dull light. In extreme close-up is a set of lips painted a bright fuchsia, plump and glistening, framing bright white teeth. The voice that comes from them has a soothing British accent. I don't recognize the voice, but whoever it is doesn't want to be known because the camera never pans away to reveal the entire face.

"Welcome," the woman says, her lips moving slowly. "You're here because you were chosen by a member sponsor to join our elite secret society. With their nomination, each of you was secretly vetted for a position. When you passed our strict requirements, an invitation was delivered to you, which brings you here tonight.

"We found each of you to be superior candidates, based on your unique social placement in your chosen professional fields. You may have something you want—success, wealth, women, men, anything your heart desires. Through our extensive secret network, in time, we can make all your dreams come true with membership in our club.

"When our members succeed, our secret society succeeds. This is a mutually beneficial relationship. But I must warn you, this exclusive opportunity comes at a very high price, something you must give us so that we may give back to you. The cost of entrance is simple. You only need answer one question to apply."

The lips disappear and the screen is replaced with one question.

CHAPTER 11

The voice continues speaking as I glare at the question written across the screen in bold letters.

WHAT'S YOUR SECRET?

"To be considered for a membership, you must reveal your greatest secret, but we don't accept just any secret. Your membership is only secured if you tell us the secret that could destroy you. You were chosen because we believe you have something to hide, but also something to give. Rest easy, your secret is safe with us as long as the club and its members' identities and their exploits remain unknown. We will protect you, if you protect us.

"When you're ready, please keystroke your secret into the touch-screen keyboard at the bottom of the monitor. After receipt, if your secret passes our requirements, you will then be considered for a position within our club. Don't worry, it's kept on a highly encrypted and secure system where only the Grand Master will have access if you break our only rule—complete secrecy."

This whole thing has caught me off guard. My greatest secret? How would they know I have anything interesting to offer?

But I realize quickly that this is merely blackmail. A piece of me, which will protect them. I look up to find Raine leaning into her screen. She's eagerly pecking out her answer with the tip of one finger.

"Are you seriously going to do it?" I ask incredulously. Raine glances up at me with a smug smirk. "Are you crazy? This could be the story of the century."

She's so hungry for an exclusive that it's terrifying. But it also irks me because this is my story, not hers. I'm just not stupid enough to say it out loud.

When she finishes, I'm still thinking. This is not something to jump into lightly. My secret could destroy my life and the people I love, but apparently it could give me everything I want, all the things that Alex has. And most importantly, the secure life that I've wanted for Hayden— the best doctors, a house, the best schooling, anything he needs or wants. I wouldn't have to be that single mom who struggles. Doing this could give him everything.

All for just one price.

I stop my mind before it goes there. It's wrong to take a shortcut, but at the same time I'm conflicted. For so long I've waited on the sidelines, watching Alex receive everything she wants by doing almost nothing. To this day, I blame her and Casper for the fact that we lost Angelface, even though I bear an equal blame. By sleeping with each other behind my back, they destroyed the amazing business I built from the ground up. Yet I was the one to pay the price and come out empty-handed. After all this time, jealousy still tastes bitter on my tongue.

Quickly, I wage an internal battle, debating over right and wrong. My good half reasons with me. I remind myself that I'm here for the story, not the benefits. I'll be working hard until I get the story and the job at Z. Doing things the right way means I can raise Hayden the way he deserves to be raised, by a good mother who deserves him.

Whatever the reason I settle on in my mind, I choose to move forward. Either way I look at this situation, it's a win-win if no one will ever learn my secret. With trembling fingers, I tap the information on the screen's digital keyboard—the secret that I've kept for years. The one thing I thought I would keep hidden until my dying day.

After a deep breath, I press ENTER and the form fades away, replaced by the fuchsia lips.

"Congratulations. Your applications have been received."

A secret compartment in the shape of a circle drops away from the table and a pair of sparkling champagne glasses ascend from beneath.

"Please pick up your glasses," requests the lips.

I pick up the glass closest to me, and Raine picks up hers.

"A toast. May your truth raise you and not destroy you."

We lift our glasses in the air. Everything's happening too fast for me, but apparently not for Raine. She's already downing her drink.

"Oh my, it's Dom." She tips her glass back, finishing in seconds.

"Aren't you worried that it's drugged or something?"

"Lady, I don't know who you are, but didn't you just hand over your most guarded secret?"

I nod.

"Well, I'm not sure about you, but if my secret leaks, I'd want to be dead. Who the hell cares what they do to me now?"

Sadly, she has a point. Would they concoct all this to kill us? No. I want to believe that this is legitimate. Alex must have gone through this too, and the thought gives me some sense of ease.

I relent and take a tiny sip. The champagne tastes normal; no odd aftertaste. I'm a little more than half done when a sickening coldness begins to creep over me, starting with my toes. My eyes widen as it travels up my legs, circles my stomach, and catapults out my numbing arms. Black spots develop in front of my eyes, and a concerned-looking Raine disappears behind blackness as the spots grow and obscure my eyesight.

My muscles relax and my fingers unwillingly release the glass, tipping it out of my hand. I can't stop the remaining champagne from pouring onto the floor, because that's when I lose complete control of my body and black out.

veryone's laughing.

It's like a terrible nightmare that I can't escape. My forehead's sweating as sunlight, I think, warms my face, making the inside of my eyelids glow pink. As I'm slowly coming to, I wipe my palm over my mouth. It's wet. I'm drooling and my throat is dry, making me cough.

Everyone laughs louder.

Or maybe they're laughing the same, but I'm waking up. I squint my eyes, opening them one at a time. Fuzzy shapes slowly solidify into people I recognize, but no one I'm interested in seeing. Casey, Jackson, Olivia, Brent, and all the other people in the office whose names I haven't memorized yet.

"I think she's wearing the same clothes as yesterday." Casey giggles.

I gasp and sit up, my eyes wide as I try to remember what the hell happened. Even though my coworkers are having fun at my expense, I ignore them and lean over my desk, trying to rub away my pulsing headache with a shaky hand.

Pushing into my memories, I find only fragments of

distorted flashes of imagery—the warehouse district at night, the limo, giving my secret away, the club, and the champagne. That's it; it must have been the champagne. I must have been drugged, and now I'm here at the office. A wave of nausea sweeps over me, making me shaky because I can't account for anything in between then and now, which I believe is at least eight hours. And I have no idea how I ended up at the office.

I groan.

"You okay?"

Squinting, I glance up to find Vega standing next to my desk. His dark eyes are warm with concern as they search mine. He holds out a small white paper cup, the size used for Jell-O shooters.

"Café Cubano," he says, and moves the offering closer.

"Thanks." I accept the sweet espresso shot and down it. If this doesn't pick me up, nothing in this world will.

"So you worked all night?" He looks me over, his brow furrowed.

I look down at myself and realize that Casey was right; I am wearing the same clothes as yesterday. They're very rumbled and I feel disheveled, but not sick. I take a moment to take a mental tally of my body—feet, legs, arms, chest, head—all here, all feeling fine, just groggy and confused, but I'm okay and safe. That's the good news.

"Yeah. Worked all night." My voice breaks as I lie. With slow movements, I crack my stiff neck, then brush back my messy hair with my palms and straighten my top, trying in vain to pull myself together. I'm at work, and my crush is staring at me.

"Your story, right? You found something good?" Vega presses.

Out of the corner of my eye, I notice Casey being very quiet and attentive at her desk next to mine, and I remember Vega's warning yesterday. Trust no one. There's no way I'll let her steal my story. It's bad enough that I have to compete with Raine Whitezman, the award-winning journalist from the most popular local news channel in Miami. She's a professional, not just some cocky intern. If the pressure wasn't on before, it certainly is now.

"You could say that."

"Sorry to interrupt." A new voice joins our chat. Tandy, the woman who originally hired me, appears in my line of sight and turns to Vega. "I need to meet with you over the Diaz story—lunch?" She reaches out, twisting her fingers around his cord necklace, and though everything's still hazy, I think she's flirting with him. Or seducing him.

No fraternizing, my ass.

Since I started, I've learned she's the owner's daughter, and according to my intern besties, she and Vega dated until about six months ago. She's been quickly working her way up the office ladder, ruffling feathers in her spoiled wake.

Jackson rolls his chair into my cubicle and leans in close. "There's no way you can compete with that," he offers in hushed tones as he eyes Tandy, who is just as beautiful and perfect as everyone else in this town. She's Jamaican, with smooth tawny skin, wild crystal-blue eyes, and an accent that even turns me on.

"Who says I'm trying?"

"No one has to, sweetheart. The sexual tension between you and Vega is *muy caliente.*" He presses his finger into my arm and hisses a burning sound, right before he rolls back into his cube.

Little jerk.

He's right, though. I can't compete, even if there is something *caliente* between Vega and me, or perhaps the heat is only on my end. Not only is Tandy gorgeous, but she'll probably run Z News one day. She has more to offer than I ever will.

She whispers in his ear, her bronze-colored curls brushing against his cheek. But he's looking over her shoulder and watching me. His face turns three shades of crimson at the same time she laughs. Thank God I can't hear their exchange, but unfortunately I see everything. She drags a seductive palm over his chest in a way that leaves me burning inside, and then sashays away with an ass-swaying that would put Beyoncé to shame.

I clear my throat and turn my attention to my keyboard and begin to type, even though my eyes are still slightly blurry. Anything I can do to appear busy and uninterested in their conversation.

Vega returns with another shot of café Cubano and sets it down on my desktop. "Why don't you go home for the day, maybe take a shower and a long nap?"

"No, it's okay. I'm good." I widen my dry eyes, attempting to appear more alert. I can't possibly leave now with so much at stake, and I'll need the office computers to do research on the club and everything that happened last night in the limo.

"I insist, especially since you're typing and your computer isn't even turned on." He chuckles, pats the computer top twice, and walks away.

"Damn it," I say under my breath. The monitor wasn't even facing him. How did he know?

Casey and Jackson snicker from their cubicles, but I don't bother engaging them. Instead, because it seems like I really don't have a choice in the matter, I gather my things, including my purse, which all miraculously made it here with me, and I leave. I do need a shower, and I need to piece together what the hell happened last night.

Five minutes later I'm in the building's parking garage, realizing that I left my car in the warehouse district. At least, that's what I remember last.

I lift my purse, unzip it, and riffle through, looking for my phone to call a taxi. Instead, I find two things that don't belong to me. One is a fancy silver compact with Raine's name engraved on the front. I'm not sure how it came to be in my handbag, but I can't worry about that right now.

The other item is a set of keys that I don't recognize. A keyless car remote hangs from them. I inspect them, wondering if they belong to Alex. With her constant disorganization, our belongings are always getting mixed up. I press the button and in response, a car's alarm beeps, echoing off the enclosed concrete walls.

I continue pressing the button as I search the parking garage for the car it matches. When I find it, it's a black Audi A7. My dream car, the one I always knew I would never afford but still dreamed about, regardless.

At the driver's side, I lean over the hood and snag the onyx envelope secured beneath the windshield wiper. I flip it over and rip open the flap. Inside is a thick card, one side bright fuchsia like the lips in my memory, and the other side black.

Unlike before, there's something written on the card. The hot-pink script reads WELCOME TO THE MIAMI HUSH CLUB

CHAPTER 13

This time, as soon as I read and comprehend the card, the edges of the paper singe as though they're being burned but without fire. They curl and roll until the paper shrivels to ash in my hands. I stare at it, completely dumbfounded as to how it happened. What's left of the tiny pieces sifts between my fingers, fluttering to the garage floor. The only proof that the card ever existed is an empty black envelope and the black smudge marks on my hand.

I spin around, looking to see if anyone saw what I just witnessed, but there's no one here. Only a brand new car for which I assume with confusion is for me.

I don't return home right away. Instead, I drive the Audi to the warehouse district, looking for my old Honda. Though I've checked the glove box in the Audi and all the papers say that I own it, which is strangely exciting and terrifying because the papers all have my signature, but I have no recollection of signing anything.

What the hell have I gotten myself into that merits receiving a car as a gift with entry to a club? When the mysterious woman claimed they'd make my dreams come true, I can't say that I completely believed her, but the little that I do remember from last night just became a little more real.

In the daylight, the warehouse district doesn't look as menacing. Workers are loading trucks with boxes or making deliveries. When I arrive where I parked my car last night, it's no longer there. I pull into a space, turn off the Audi, and step out in the sunshine. I search the ground as if this will give me some clue as to where "they" have taken it, though I'm not really sure it matters, or who "they" really are.

But the most concerning part is that being here sparks absolutely no memories from last night after passing out in the limo. Where did they take me? What did they do to me? Who took me back to the office?

I slide my Dollar Store shades over my eyes and cross my arms over my chest, evaluating the area. No one is watching me as I look around, which is a good thing, I think. I admit my sleuthing may need some work; I'm still just an intern, after all.

I pull out my phone and stare at the numbers, ready to press 911, thinking I should file a report with the police for my missing car. But that would lead to a shit-ton of questions that I can't answer, and would probably get me kicked out of the club that may win me my dream job— not just my dream car.

So I drop my cell phone back into my pocket and slide into the car, feeling somewhat smug about finally having functioning air-conditioning in the ninety-degree heat with eighty-five percent humidity. As I head home, I enjoy the easy ride, the smell of the buttery leather seats, and the rocking sound system more than I care to admit. I should feel extremely guilty for liking everything about this, but it's easier to lie to myself and say it's all to get the story, which is exactly what I do.

After I park in our building's garage, I ride the elevator to the twenty-sixth floor and make my way to the condo. Inside, Alex is on the balcony smoking a Cuban cigar and sipping a martini while looking out at the city skyline. The radio is blasting with her favorite song, "Hotel California." I hate this song, and she knows it.

"For a model, you sure do a lot of bad things." I toss my handbag on a nearby chair and walk out onto the balcony. "I invented bad things, big sister." She smiles behind huge designer sunglasses, then says, "This came for you," as she holds out a black envelope.

"Thanks." I reluctantly accept the envelope. It's exactly like the one left on my new car.

"I can't believe you actually had the cojones to do it."

I stop at the door and turn to chat with her, but Alex is still looking out over the city, taking a drag from her cigar, then slowly exhaling a ribbon of smoke that's picked up by the breeze.

"You know when I decide on something I want," I say as I cross my arms over my chest, "I go for it."

"I know, but it required you to give up something very

important." She swivels, lowers her glasses, and looks up at me with a suspicious gaze.

"It did."

She's hinting at my secret. I don't want to talk about it or even think of it in her presence. My sister knows me so well, she may somehow hear the words slipping through the barriers in my mind. We both have things we hide from each other, even though I would still consider her my closest friend. Thankfully, before this unwanted conversation goes any further, someone knocks on the front door, saving me.

"He's here!" Alex jumps up with uncharacteristic excitement and strides across the condo in her red bikini. She swings open the door and says in her sexiest voice, "Hello, darling."

I expect to see her sugar daddy, Marco, but instead, I suck in a quick ragged breath at who's actually standing there—my ex-boyfriend and old business partner, the guy who shattered my heart and cheated on me with Alex.

Casper Dunn.

Casper. Fucking. Dunn.

To be continued . . .

INTERACT

If you enjoyed this episode of the MIAMI HUSH CLUB, please take a moment to write a spoiler-free review on the site where you purchased the book. By sharing your feelings in a review, on your blog, on social media, or with a friend about the book, you support this independent author.

 Please join Michelle Warren's mailing list to learn about future novels and sales. Use the your QR code scanner to open the form and join, or use this link: http://tinyurl.com/pkqhspl

Would you like to see the Miami Hush Club as a movie or TV series?
Show your support by clicking "supported" and also help select the cast here:
http://iflist.com/stories/miamihushclub#

Add pins to the Miami Hush Club
Pinterest board:
https://www.pinterest.com/michellewarren/miami-hush-club-book/

WANT TO JOIN THE MIAMI HUSH CLUB?
Enter your secret here for an exclusive invitation.
http://tinyurl.com/obp65fg

ACKNOWLEDGMENTS

A big thank-you goes out to my beautiful, amazing, and totally badass beta readers. They've suffered through incomplete error-ridden drafts that bear no resemblance to the final product. Thank you for telling me when I suck, because you only make me better. I love you, ladies!

Lisa Anthony
Amy Bettwy
Pamela Carrion
Megan Hickey Kapusta
Jen Lowe
Nikki Shaw
Laura Wilson
and Leslie Sanchez for her translations.

Pam Berehulke from Bulletproof Editing is my extraordinarily kind, patient, and talented editor. I want to tell every author about her, but also hide her away because I want to keep her all to myself. I'm greedy that way. Thank you, Pam, for your awesomeness!

And to my husband, Warren (the namesake of my pen name), who always gets the short end of the stick. I owe you for all the evenings you sucked it up with takeout (though you know any food is better than what I cook), and the nights you gave up and went to bed without me while I tapped away on your laptop. You handed over our precious time so I could pursue my passion. You and our love inspire me.

CONNECT

FIND MORE INFO ONLINE AT:

MICHELLE-WARREN.COM

TSU.CO:

www.tsu.co/MichelleWarren

TWITTER:

www.twitter.com/@MMichelleWarren

INSTAGRAM:

www.instagram.com/MMichelleWarren

PINTEREST:

www.pinterest.com/michellewarren

GOODREADS:

https://www.goodreads.com/author/show/4097828.Michelle_Warren

FACEBOOK:

www.facebook.com/MichelleWarrenAuthor

GOOGLEPLUS:

plus.google.com/u/0/+MichelleWarrenAuthor/posts

JOIN MY MAILING LIST:

HTTP://TINYURL.COM/PKQHSPL

ABOUT THE AUTHOR

Michelle Warren didn't travel the road to writer immediately, first she spent over a decade as a professional illustrator and designer. Her artistic creativity combined with her love of science fiction, paranormal, and fantasy led her to write her first YA novel, *Wander Dust*. Michelle loves reading and traveling to places that inspire her to create. She lived in Miami for six years, which inspired this book, but currently resides in downtown Chicago.

BOOKS BY MICHELLE WARREN INCLUDE:

MIAMI HUSH CLUB
Episode 1 | Episode 2 | Episode 3 | Episode 4

HE + SHE

THE SERAPHINA PARRISH TRILOGY
Wander Dust
Protecting Truth
Seeing Light

COMING SOON!
Mr. Right Now
Sugar Skulls

Made in the USA
Charleston, SC
08 January 2015